A NOTE ABOUT THE STORY

During a summer spent in Sweden, Carole Lexa Schaefer witnessed firsthand many of the traditional elements of the Midsummer celebration that inspired this tale. She tells us that one of the most important and colorful elements of Swedish *Midsomor* festivities is the *majstang*, or Maypole. Despite appearances, the word has nothing to do with the month of May. It means "to decorate with green leaves and branches," which are often taken from birch trees. Maypoles, houses, and even boats and automobiles are decorated with garlands of leaves and flowers. Sometimes a special decoration, such as a rooster, a crown of flowers, a long banner, or a little sailboat, is placed on top of the Maypole.

Under shade trees, somewhere near the Maypole, coffee and dinner tables are set with pretty cloths, flowers, and plenty of good things to eat.

During the evening hours, young and old people join hands to sing and dance around the Maypole, often accompanied by the music of fiddles and accordions. Around midnight, the sun drops below the horizon. In the far north, it stays down only a few moments, then up it rises. Farther south, this *skyming*, or twilight time, lasts longer. But all over Sweden it is a magical time that some claim is a sure cure for grouchiness—and even old age.

When I first saw the oil paintings of Pat Geddes I was struck with the magic in her use of light, and both the innocence and complexity of her naive style. Through her sunny illustrations and Carole Schaefer's gentle story we hope to give readers a taste of the light and warmth expressed by the people of Sweden during their treasured celebration of summer.

Tomie dePaola, Creative Director
WHITEBIRD BOOKS

Under the Midsummer Sky

CAROLE LEXA SCHAEFER

ILLUSTRATED BY

PAT GEDDES

A WHITEBIRD BOOK
G. P. Putnam's Sons
New York

Text copyright © 1994 by Carole Lexa Schaefer. Illustrations copyright © 1994 by Pat Geddes
All rights reserved. This book, or parts thereof, may not be reproduced
in any form without permission in writing from the publisher. G. P. Putnam's Sons,
a division of The Putnam & Grosset Group, 200 Madison Avenue, New York, NY 10016.
G. P. Putnam's Sons, Reg. U.S. Pat. & Tm. Off. Published simultaneously in Canada.
Printed in Hong Kong by South China Printing Co. (1988) Ltd.
Book design by Gunta Alexander. The text is set in Kennerley.
Library of Congress Cataloging-in-Publication Data
Schaefer, Carole Lexa.   Under the midsummer sky: a Swedish folktale/
by Carole Lexa Schaefer; illustrated by Pat Geddes.   p. cm.
Summary: When Mohma and Pohpa try to surprise each other at Midsummer, the results
turn out a little different than intended. [1. Folklore—Sweden.] I. Geddes, Pat, ill.
II. Title. PZ8.1.S294Un 1993 398.2—dc20 [E] 91-38157 CIP AC
ISBN 0-399-21858-0
1 3 5 7 9 10 8 6 4 2

To all the dancing Lexas—especially Ruth and Frank.
And to Karin.—C.L.S.

To my daughters Ann, Mary, and Jane —P.G.

Far up north, where summer nights are long and bright, Mohma and Pohpa lived in a red wooden house between the forest and the sea.

One morning they stood in their garden shooing away crows. "Those rascally birds love all this light. They won't go away till nights are dark again," Pohpa complained.

"Well, crows are the only darkness we'll see today," said Mohma. "It's Midsummer."

Pohpa flopped down on the garden bench. "Bah, Midsummer," he grumbled. "The longest day of the year."
Pohpa mopped his forehead with his big handkerchief.

Mohma walked slowly into the henhouse.

As she gathered up eggs, she spoke to the chickens. "My pretty chicks," she said, "our Pohpa's working too hard. What he needs is the fun of a Midsummer Maypole."

"Cut-cut-cuh *dut*," clucked the chickens.

"Sh-h. Don't tell," Mohma whispered. "I'm going to surprise him."

Into her basket, along with the eggs, Mohma tucked
a little hatchet and a cloth sack. She walked across the
yard to the garden.

"Pohpa," she said, "the hens laid so many eggs today, I'm going down the road to sell them. Folks like extra eggs for their Midsummer feasts."

Pohpa watched her go out the front gate and across the meadow.

"Phuff, I'm such a grouch," he muttered to Esme
the goat as he trudged into the milking shed. "Mohma
deserves some feasting today herself. I'm going to see
that she gets it."

"Ma-a-a," Esme bleated.

"Hush now," said Pohpa. "It's a secret."

Carrying a pail of milk into the house, he said, "Ten-egg custard—that's what she likes best."

He plunked the pail down on the kitchen table.
"Milk goes into custard—and sugar, too, I think," he said,
setting the sugar tin beside the pail.

"And fresh eggs, of course," he added, and opened the
cupboard.

"Och!" he cried. "No eggs! Mohma took them all with
her!"

Pohpa hurried out to the henhouse. "Come on,
Hensy, Clucksy, Bertie, Gertie, Hester, Nester," he
called, coaxing the chickens by name. "You must give
me eggs."

But the chickens squawked and flapped away.

All Pohpa found was one brown egg and two
white ones.

Back in the kitchen, he stirred them in a pot on the stove. "I'll make *three*-egg custard," he said, adding only a drop of milk and just a pinch of sugar.

He cooked and stirred and cooked and stirred. "Hm-m. This doesn't look much like Mohma's custard, but plenty of wild strawberries will pretty it up."

While Pohpa worked, Mohma was busy too—but not selling eggs. She filled her sack with meadow flowers. Then she walked among the slender birch trees at the edge of the forest.

"To make a Maypole, I need a tree trunk with its branches trimmed off," she said. "But why should I fuss with all that chopping when there are plenty of nice sticks lying about?"

She stood one up in the grass. "Um-hmm. Smooth enough to decorate and tall enough to dance around," she said with a curtsy and a twirl.

Back at home, in the front yard, Mohma called, "Hallo-o, Pohpa." There was no answer.

"Good, he's busy with something—probably those old crows," she said, and stuck the birch stick into the ground.

Onto the stick, she tied an old broom handle for a crosspiece with two twigs to brace it. "This will have to do," she said.

Next, she wove the flowers into two wreaths. But when she hung them on the broom handle—it tilted.

One wreath fell off. Mohma laid the other in the grass.

"I guess this isn't tied right," she said, loosening
the rope.

Just then she heard Pohpa calling from the garden,
"Hallo-o, Mohma."

"Oh, no!" she cried, looking at the bare lopsided
Maypole. "I must have *something* on this before he
sees it."

Mohma dashed into the house, grabbed a wrinkled
paper moon lantern out of the wooden chest,

and hung it on top of the Maypole.

Then, rushing off to find Pohpa, she bumped right into him.

"Oof! Where are you going so fast?" he sputtered.

"To look for you," she said.

"Well, I've been picking berries," he said, taking her hand. "Come and see."

Pohpa led Mohma around back beneath the apple
trees where he'd set a table with their best dishes, a pot
of tea, and a platter of wild strawberries.

In the middle of the platter, Mohma spied a mound of
something yellow and lumpy. "Oh, Pohpa," she cried,
"you've made us a lovely Midsummer supper—wild
strawberries and scrambled eggs!"

For a moment Pohpa stared at his three-egg custard surrounded by berries. Then he chuckled. "So I have. Would you like some?"

"Yes indeed," said Mohma.

When they'd eaten every bit, Mohma said, "Now I've something to show you."

Pohpa followed her into the front yard.

"Haw! Would you look at that," he cried, pointing in the direction of her Maypole. "You've made us a scarecrow to chase those pesky birds away!"

Mohma looked where he pointed. The wind puffed out the round moon-face of a scarecrow that smiled and waved its tilted broom handle arms.

Mohma laughed and waved back. "Yes, oh yes," she said. "It's a scarecrow for sure."

"And look here," said Pohpa, putting a wreath on each of their heads. "Flowers for us to wear."

Mohma curtsied. Pohpa bowed. And they danced far into the night under the Midsummer sky.